CHARLES DICKENS
CAPTAIN MURDERER

Pictures by Rowan Barnes-Murphy

Adapted by George Harland

Lothrop, Lee & Shepard Books
New York

For Frankie—R.B.-M.
For Yvonne—G.H.

CHARLES DICKENS was born in Portsmouth,
England, in 1812. At his death in 1870 he was
acknowledged as one of the greatest of Eng-
lish novelists. His grave is in Westminster Ab-
bey. *Captain Murderer* is a story his nurse told
him when he was a young child, which he
recorded in a book of reminiscences, *The Un-
commercial Traveller.*

Printed in the United States of America.
First Edition

1 2 3 4 5 6 7 8 9 10

Library of Congress Cataloging in Publication Data
Harland, George.   Captain Murderer.
Summary: Captain Murderer, a possible relation of the Bluebeard family, weds a series of
wealthy young girls that he then proceeds to kill and bake into a pie.
[1. Horror stories] I. Barnes-Murphy, Rowan, ill. II. Dickens, Charles, 1812–1870.
Captain Murderer. III. Title.   PZ7.H2264Cap 1986   [E]   86-2887
ISBN 0-688-06306-3   ISBN 0-688-06307-1 (lib. bdg.)

When I was a child of less than six years old, living in Chatham, I had a nursemaid called Mary Weller. I always remember Mary for her bedtime stories, and one in particular sticks in my memory. Mary delighted in the macabre and horrific, and her bedtime stories were always tinged with this. The most horrific of the stories was kept for when I was ill and, being a sickly child, I heard it many, many times. Although I knew it word for word and could repeat it with her, I couldn't resist hearing it again and again.

"Now Master Charles," she would say, "if you're a good little boy and take your lov'ly medicine, I'll tell you a nice little bedtime story."

I always fell for the ploy and would take my lov'ly medicine meekly and, tingling with excitement, my eyes closed, I would lie back on the pillows and wait.

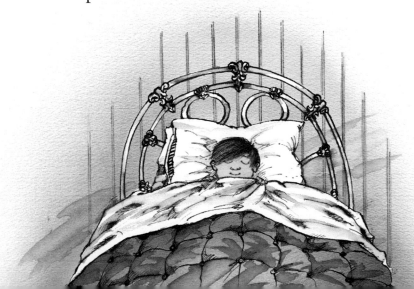

"Once upon a time, Master Charles, there was this gentleman called Captain Murderer."

Captain Murderer! He must have been an offshoot of the Bluebeard family, though I had no idea of that relationship in those days. His warning name appeared to have no effect on his neighbors, for he was admitted into the best society and possessed immense wealth. Captain Murderer's mission in life was matrimony and the gratification of a cannibal appetite with tender young brides. . . .

On his marriage morning, dear, Captain Murderer had both sides of the way to the church planted with curious flowers, and when the young bride saw them she would say, 'Dear Captain Murderer, I never saw flowers like these before. What are they called?' and he would answer, 'They are garnish for house—lamb!' and the way he laughed at his ferocious practical joke, displaying for the first time a row of very sharp teeth, had a disquieting effect on the minds of the noble bridal company, dear.

He always married in a coach and twelve, and all his noble horses were milk white except for one red spot on the back, which he caused to be hidden by the harness. For that spot *would* come there, though every horse was milk white when the Captain bought him. And that spot was young—bride's—blood, dear!

The wedding festivities went on for a whole month, and when all the guests had been dismissed and Captain Murderer was alone with his young bride, he would take out a golden rolling pin and a silver pie board. Now, there was this special feature about the Captain's courtships, dear. He would always ask if the young lady could make pie crust. If she couldn't, then she was taught.

Well, when the young bride saw Captain Murderer produce the golden rolling pin and the silver pie board, she remembered this and turned up her laced silk sleeves to make a pie. The Captain brought out an enormous silver pie dish and flour and butter and eggs and all the things needed for the pie—except for the INSIDE.

The lovely young bride saw this, dear, and she said, 'Dear Captain Murderer, what is this pie to be?'

'A meat pie!'

'But dear Captain Murderer, I see no meat.'

'Look in the mirror!'

Well, dear, the young bride looked in the mirror, but of course still she saw no meat.

The Captain roared with laughter and, suddenly frowning, he drew out his sword and ordered her to roll out the crust.

So she rolled out the crust, dropping large tears upon it all the time because he was so cross. When she had lined the dish with the crust and had cut crust to fit on the top, the Captain called out, 'I see meat in the mirror!'

And the young bride looked up just in time to see the Captain cutting off her head, dear.

He chopped her into pieces, and peppered her, and salted her, and put her in the pie, and sent it to the baker's, and ate it all, and picked the bones, dear.

Captain Murderer went on in this way, prospering exceedingly, because the young brides all bought him handsome dowries—until he came to choose a bride from twin sisters. At first he didn't know which one to choose, for though one was fair and the other dark, they were both equally beautiful. But the fair twin loved him and the dark twin hated him so, naturally, he chose the fair one.

The dark twin would have prevented the marriage if she could, but she couldn't. However, on the night before it, she stole out and climbed his garden wall and looked in at his window through a chink in the shutter. She saw him having his teeth filed sharp by the family blacksmith. Next day she listened carefully and heard him make his joke about the house-lamb.

A month after the wedding, dear, the fair twin rolled out the pastry, and Captain Murderer cut off her head and chopped her into pieces, and peppered her, and salted her, and put her in the pie, and sent it to the baker's, and ate it all, and picked the bones, dear.

Now, the dark twin had had her suspicions much increased by the filing of the Captain's teeth and again by the house-lamb joke, so putting all things together when he gave out that her sister was dead, she guessed the truth and determined to have revenge. So she went up to the Captain's house and knocked on the knocker and pulled on the bell.

When Captain Murderer came to the door, she said, 'Dear Captain Murderer, marry me next, for I always loved you and was jealous of my sister.'

Well, dear, the Captain took this as a compliment and made a polite reply, and the marriage was soon arranged. Now, on the night before it, the dark twin again climbed to his window and again she saw him having his teeth filed sharp by the family blacksmith.

When she saw this she let out such a terrible laugh at the chink in the shutter, that the Captain's blood curdled and he jumped up saying, 'Oh, dear! I hope nothing I've eaten has disagreed with me!' At that she laughed again, a still more terrible laugh, and the Captain rushed to the window and opened the shutter, but she was nimbly gone and there was no one.

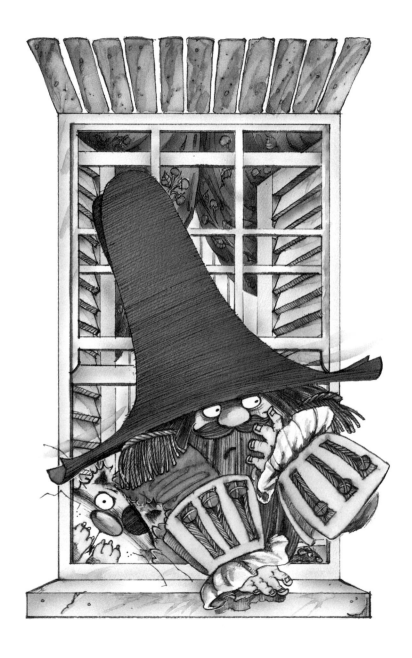

Next day they went to the church, dear, in a coach and twelve, and they were married. A month to the day later, as with all his other brides, the dark twin rolled out the pastry and Captain Murderer cut off her head, and chopped her into pieces, and peppered her, and salted her, and put her in the pie, and sent it to the baker's, and ate it all, and picked the bones, dear.

But—before she had begun to roll out the pastry the dark twin had taken a deadly poison of the most awful character, distilled from toads' eyes and spiders' knees.

Captain Murderer had hardly picked her last bone when he began to swell, and to turn blue, and to be all over spots, and to scream. And he went on swelling and turning bluer and screaming louder than ever, until he stretched from floor to ceiling and wall to wall and then, at one o'clock in the morning...

. . .he BLEW up with a loud explosion.

"Good night Master Charles, and pleasant dreams."